Fantastic Fingerprint Art

Sea Creatures

Kate Daubney

WINDMILL BOOKS

Published in 2019 by Windmill Books,
an Imprint of Rosen Publishing
29 East 21st Street, New York, NY 10010

Copyright © Arcturus Holdings Ltd, 2019

All rights reserved. No part of this book may be reproduced in any form without permission in writing from the publisher, except by a reviewer.

Illustrated by Kate Daubney
Written and edited by Susannah Bailey
Designed by Square and Circus with Emma Randall

Cataloging-in-Publication Data

Names: Daubney, Kate.
Title: Sea creatures / Kate Daubney.
Description: New York : Windmill Books, 2019. | Series: Fantastic fingerprint art
Identifiers: LCCN ISBN 9781508195313 (pbk.) | ISBN 9781508195306 (library bound) | ISBN 9781508195320 (6 pack)
Subjects: LCSH: Fingerprints in art--Juvenile literature. | Marine animals in art--Juvenile literature. | Drawing--Technique--Juvenile literature.
Classification: LCC NC825.F55 D38 2019 | DDC 743.6--dc23

Manufactured in the United States of America

CPSIA Compliance Information: Batch BS18WM:
For Further Information contact Rosen Publishing, New York, New York at 1-800-237-9932

FINGERPRINTING IS FUN!

In this book, you'll learn how to paint your very own fingerprint sea creatures. To do this, you'll need to use different parts of your fingers.

OUR TOP TIPS:

1. Make sure you have a wet cloth or tissues nearby to change the paint on your finger.

2. Only add a tiny amount of water to your paints, or they'll become too runny.

3. Experiment with how much paint you put on your finger. The smaller the amount of paint, the quicker the print will dry!

4. Leave your prints to dry before you add any line work with a black pen.

5. You may find it easier to make some prints by turning the page around or upside down.

CLEVER CUTTLEFISH

Try painting this cunning cuttlefish.

1

2

3

4

5

6

HANDY OCTOPUS

Here's how to turn a handprint into an octopus!

WILD SEAWEED

Add fingerprint air pockets to this handprint seaweed.

PECKING PARROT FISH

Bring out your brightest paints for this brilliant reef fish!

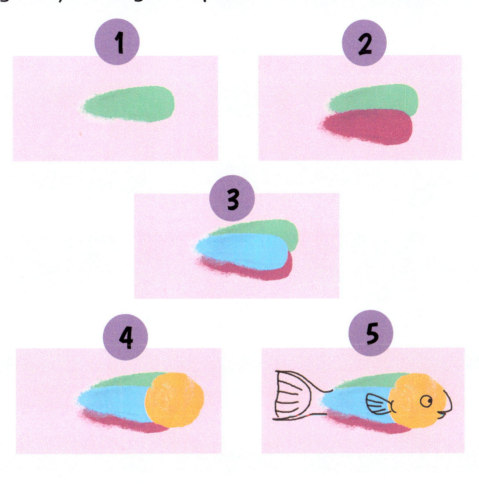

Here's a simpler baby to make.

PERFECT PUFFER FISH

Here's how to make a spotted puffer fish.

Now the puffer fish has swollen up into a spiky ball!

CLEVER CLOWN FISH

Use orange and white paint to build a stripy clown fish.

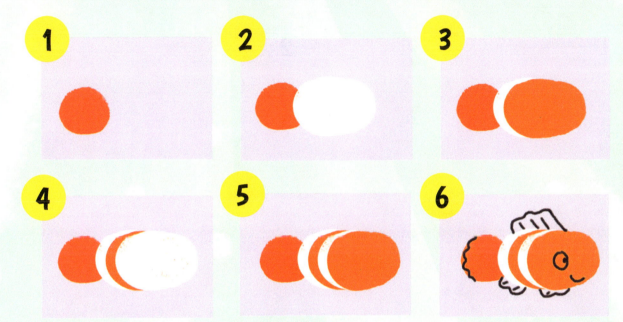

Now, use handprints to make an anemone home for your clown fish.

FANTASTIC FAN CORAL

Add branches of smudges to a handprint for this bright coral.

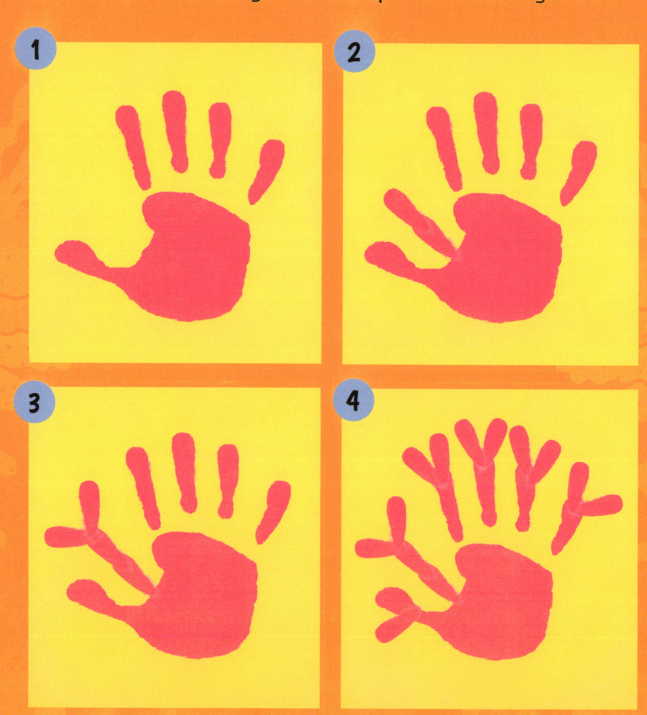

WONDERFUL WALRUS

Here's how to create a cool Arctic animal.

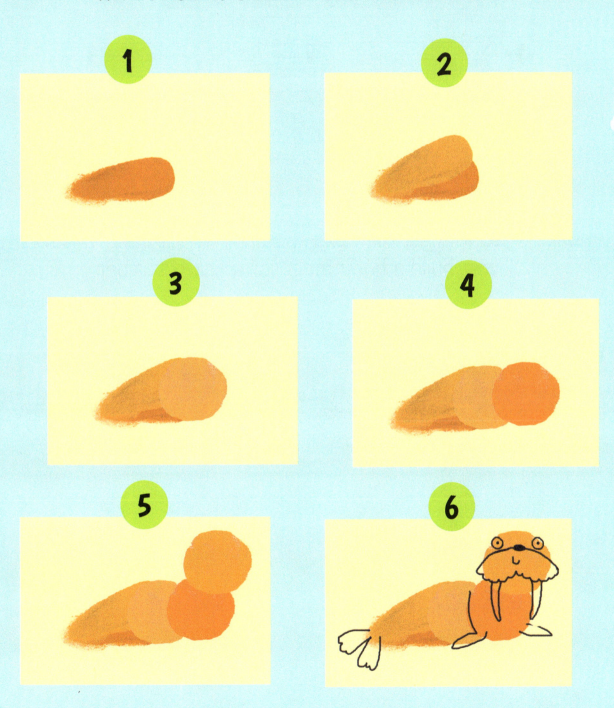

SLIMY SEA CREATURES

Try printing a simple sea slug.

Now, build a body for a spiky sea cucumber.

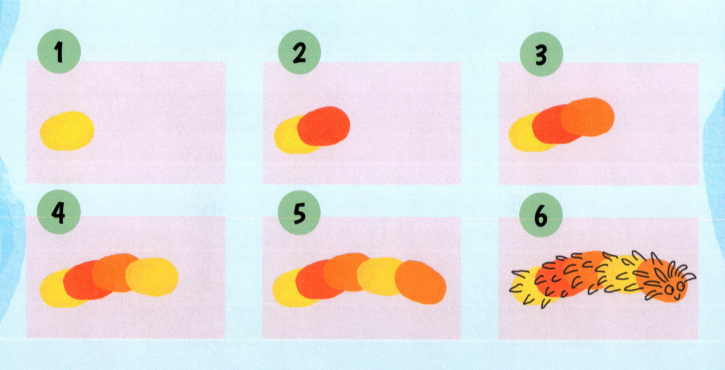

TERRIFIC TURTLES

Paint a bright fingerprint shell for a sea turtle.

1
2
3
4
5
6

Now, build a baby!

1
2
3
4

SPLENDID STARFISH

Use five golden smudges to build a body for a starfish.

SUPERB SEAHORSE

Make a simple seahorse with fins and a curly tail.

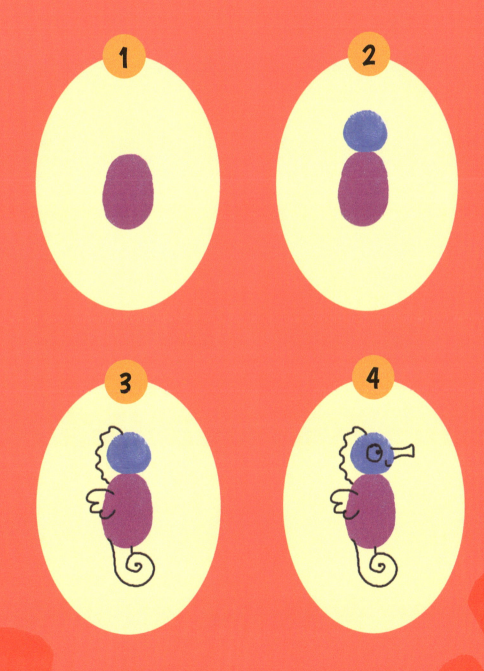

HERMIT CRAB

A tower of fingerprints makes a happy shell home for this crab.

HUGE HUMPBACKS

Here's how to make a humpback whale.

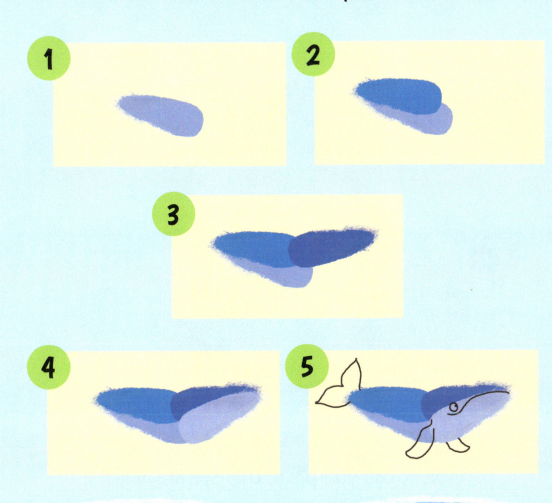

Give your grown-up whale a cute baby calf!

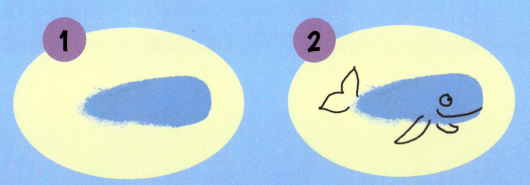

SPECIAL SEASHELLS

Here's how to make a clever cockleshell.

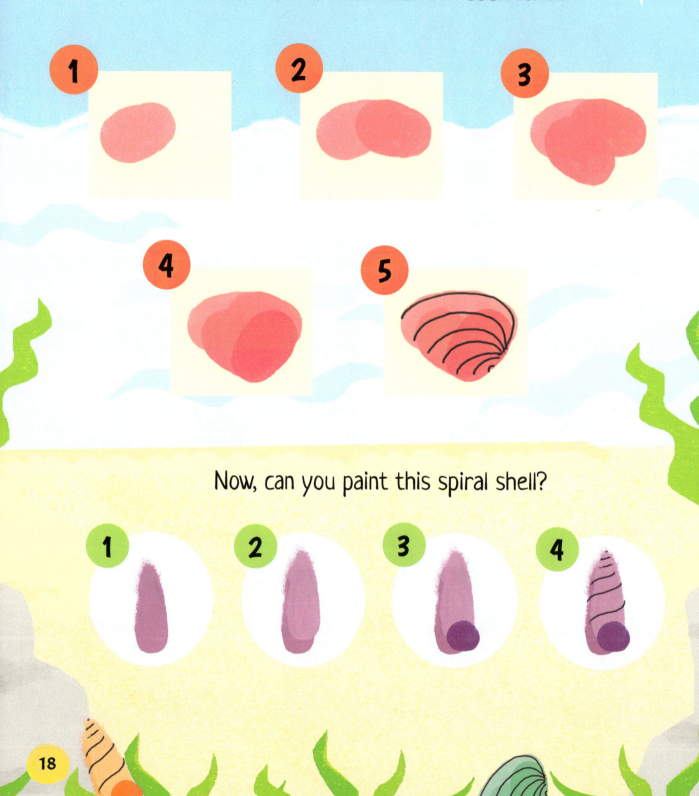

Now, can you paint this spiral shell?

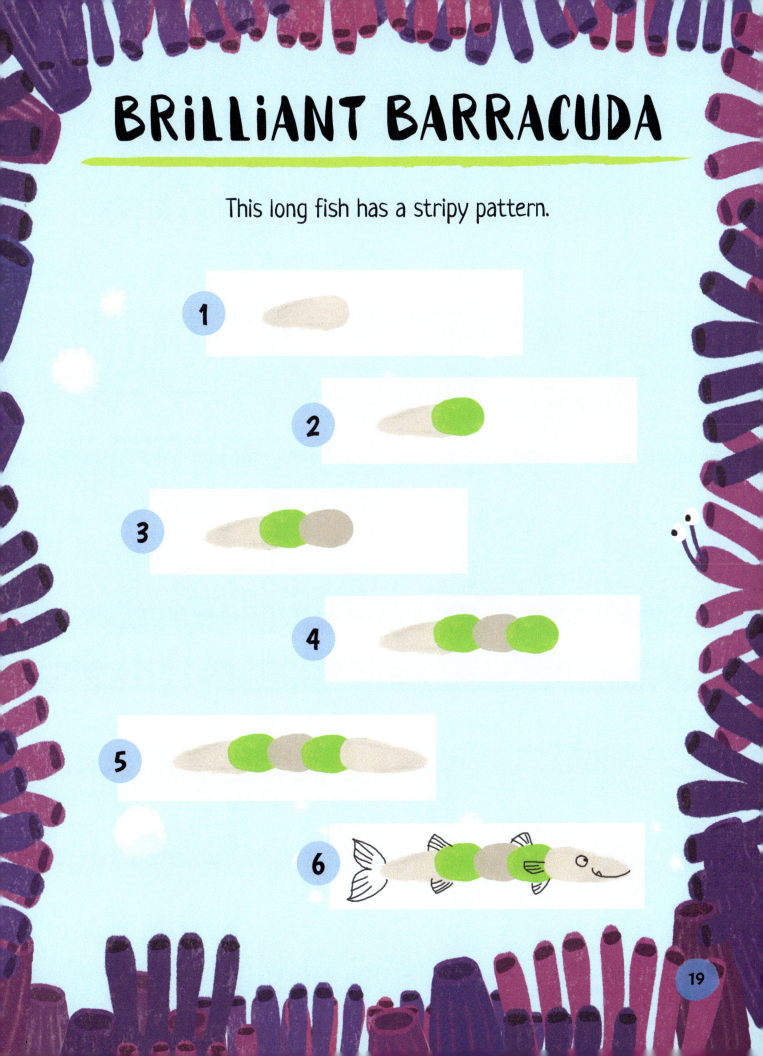

SPIKY SEA URCHINS

Can you use thumbprints to paint a spotted sea urchin?

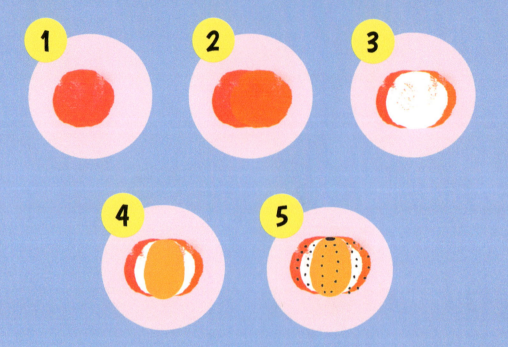

Use different paint and lines to make a spiky urchin.

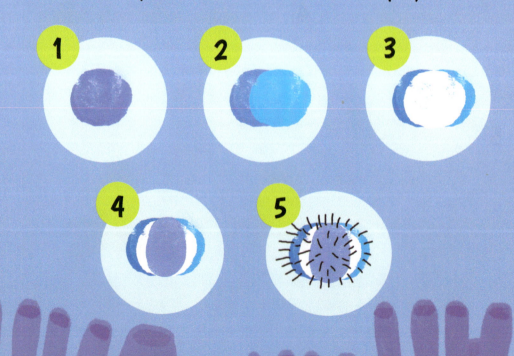

MARINE IGUANA

Make a magical marine iguana from a row of fingerprints.

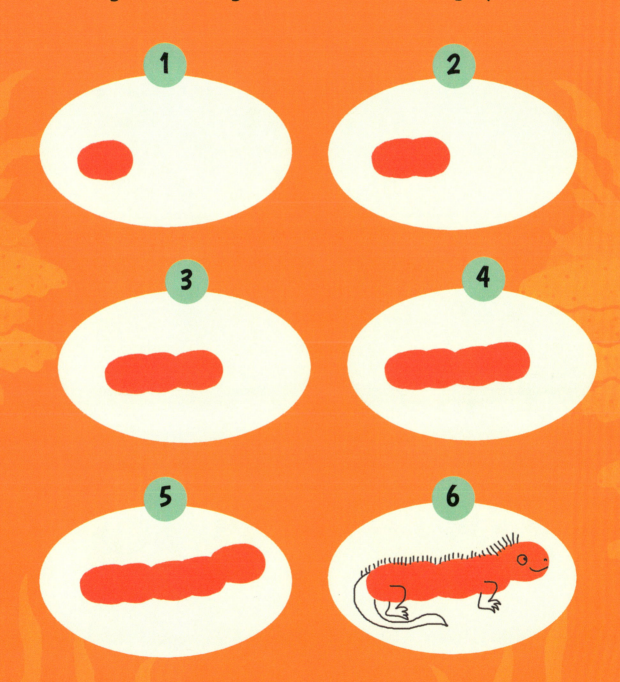

JOLLY JELLYFISH

Turn three thumbprints into a blobby jellyfish.

SPIKY LIONFISH

Use an open and closed handprint to start a fancy fish.

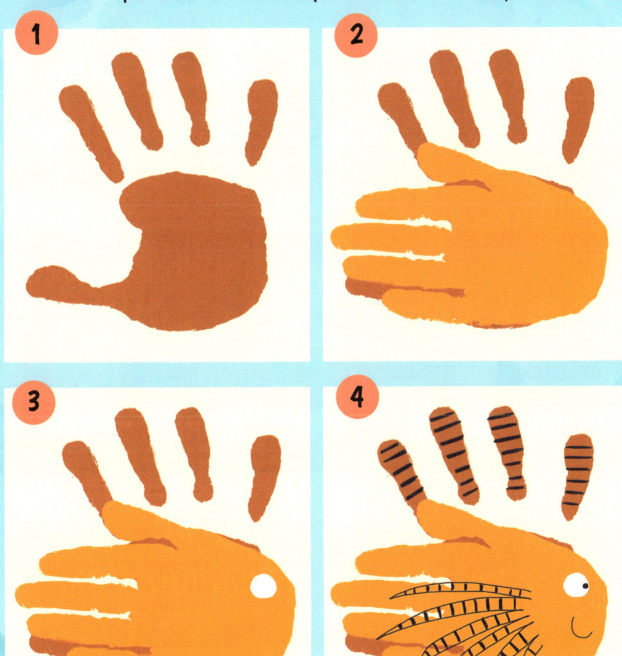

PERKY PENGUINS

Use your finger and thumb for this standing penguin.

Now, make a simple swimming penguin.

DAZZLING DOLPHINS

Follow the steps to make a diving dolphin.

Now, make a young dolphin to follow its mother.

SLIPPERY SEALS

This super seal is simple to make.

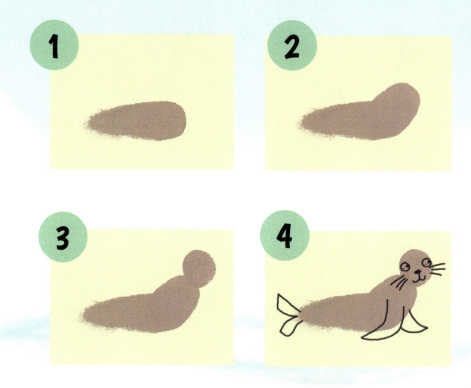

Here's how to make a cute seal pup, too.

CLEVER CLAMS

Turn a fan of smudges into a super clamshell.

1
2
3
4
5
6

Try this simple clam with a pearl inside.

1
2
3
4

LOVABLE LOBSTER

Build a body and claws for this snappy creature.

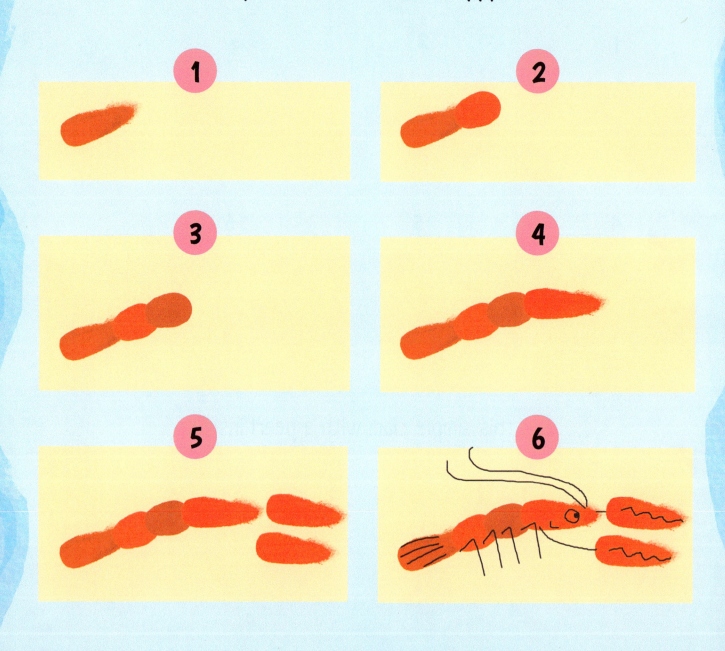

SEA OTTER

Here's how to make a swimming sea otter.

HORNED NARWHAL

This weird Arctic whale has a tusk like a horn!

1.
2.
3.
4.
5.
6.

COOL CORAL SNAKE

A curving trail of fingerprints makes a super sea snake.

FURTHER INFORMATION

Books
Balart, Maite. *Fingerprint & Draw: Animals and Insects.*
  Lake Forest, CA: Walter Foster Jr, 2017.
Martin, Jorge. *Painty Prints: Pictures to Complete with Painty Fingertips.*
  London, UK: Buster Books, 2016.
Rizzo, Johnna. *Ocean Animals: Who's Who in the Deep Blue.*
  Washington, DC: National Geographic, 2016.

Websites
For web resources related to the subject of this book, go to: www.windmillbooks.com/weblinks and select this book's title.

INDEX

barracuda 19

clam 27
clown fish 9
coral 10
crab 16
cuttlefish 4

dolphin 25

jellyfish 22

lionfish 23
lobster 28

narwhal 30

octopus 5

parrot fish 7
penguin 24
puffer fish 8

sea otter 29
sea slug 12
sea urchin 20
seahorse 15
seal 26
seashell 18

seaweed 6
shark 21
starfish 14
stingray 31

turtle 13

walrus 11
whale 17